Brooks, Erik, 1972-
The practically perfect pajamas / written and illustrated by Erik Brooks
p.   cm.
Summary: Percy gives up his beloved footed pajamas after the other polar bears tease him about them,
but then he realizes how useful they were.
ISBN 1-890817-22-8
[1. Pajamas Fiction. 2. Polar bear Fiction. 3. Bears Fiction.]
I. Title. II. Title: Practically perfect pajamas.
PZ7.B7935Pr   2000
[E] — dc21
99-16879   CIP

The illustrations in this book was prepared with watercolors and colored pencils.

Library of Congress catalog card number: 99-16879
Creative Director: Bretton Clark
Designed by Billy Kelly
Letter Art by Jessica Wolk-Stanley
Printed in Belgium

This book has a trade reinforced binding.
3 5 7 9 10 8 6 4 2

Discover worldwide links, games, activities, and more at our interactive Web site:

www.winslowpress.com

The Practically Perfect Pajamas

For Sarah

The Practically Perfect Pajamas

Written and Illustrated by

Erik Brooks

WINSLOW PRESS

DELRAY BEACH, FLORIDA • NEW YORK

Percy loved his footed pajamas more than anything else in the world. They were perfect for reading the morning paper, ideal when enjoying an afternoon snack, and a cozy necessity for a good night's sleep.

His pajamas protected his beautiful white coat from icicles between his toes, from spills when he was clumsy, and from too much shivering while he was taking a nap.

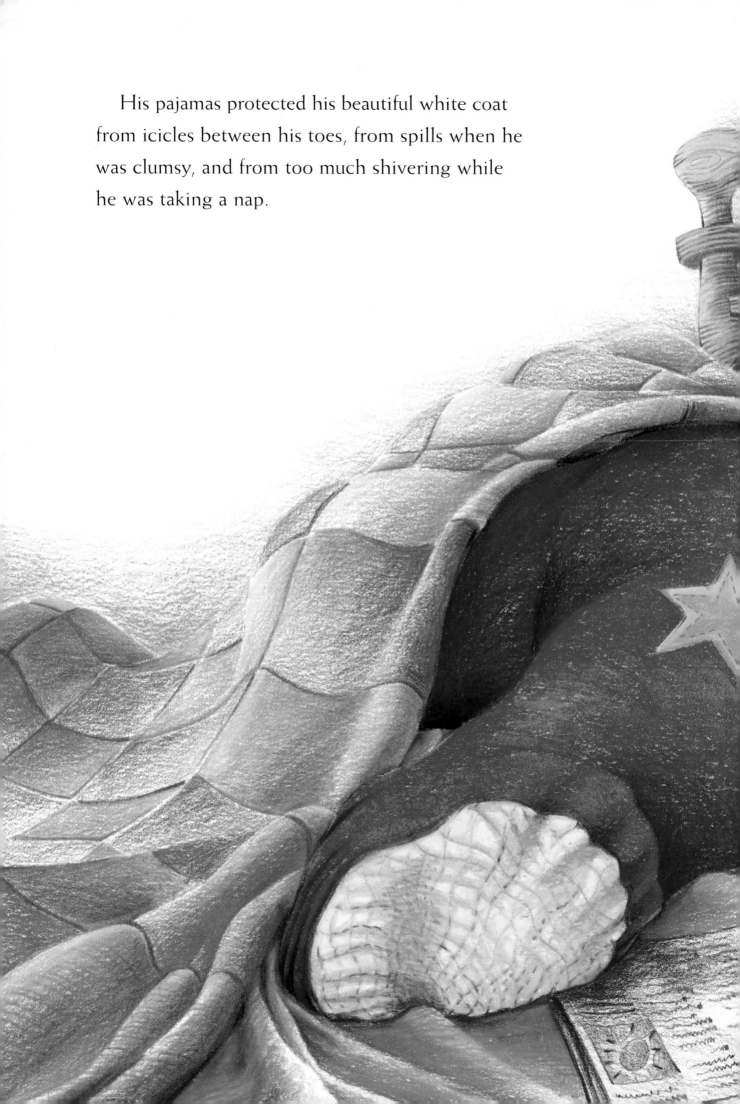

Unfortunately, Percy's pj's were only practically perfect.
Not everyone liked his pajamas as much as he did.

"Hey, fancy pants," said one bear.

"Where's the circus?" said another.

"Why can't you be more like the rest of us?"
shouted a third.

The bears teased him endlessly, and the other animals kept their distance.

Even the Arctic foxes, who are well known for following polar bears, never followed Percy.

"A bear dressed like *that*?" they chuckled. "We don't want anything to do with him."

Percy was all alone—or so he thought.

Aurora was one Arctic fox who couldn't stay away. She loved Percy's stylish pajamas, and admired that he was brave enough to be different.

"I don't care what anyone else thinks," she said. "There is nothing silly about Percy or his pj's."

One morning Percy decided that he'd had enough.
"My pajamas are great," he sighed, "but this teasing
has got to stop. Practically perfect just isn't good enough."

Reluctantly he boxed up his pajamas and put them
away forever. "Perhaps now the others will like me," he said
to himself and headed outside.

Aurora was surprised when Percy appeared without his pj's. "What can he be up to?" she said to herself. "I'd better keep an eye on him today."

A lifetime in footed pajamas had not prepared Percy for his new journey into the Arctic. He waded through several icy pools of melting snow. "This isn't so b-b-b-a-ad," he said, shivering, even though his tender feet were suffering. "Ouch. Ooooh," Percy yelped. The soft furry pads and hairs between his toes froze quickly to the ice.

"Hey, can anybody help me?" Percy called out. "My feet are stuck!" Several bears glanced in his direction, but no one came to his rescue. Instead, they simply shook their heads and wandered away.

"I wouldn't be here right now if I had my pj's," Percy whimpered. After several painful tries, he wrenched his feet loose and retreated to his den.

While his paws were thawing, Percy tried to cheer up over a late morning snack. He was feeling much better, until he accidentally bumped his cocoa. The thick chocolate syrup erupted from his mug and landed right in his lap, leaving a giant stain on his beautiful white coat.

"How can this be happening?" he said. "This is
supposed to be a perfect day."

Percy grabbed a brush and scrubbed his fur, trying to get clean.
It was impossible work. The scrubbing only spread the cocoa deeper
into his coat. Exhausted, he slumped to the floor.

"I think I need a good nap," he said.

Without his pajamas, however, sleeping was impossible, too. No matter what—left side, right side, upside, or downside—Percy could not get comfortable.

"Maybe some fresh air will do me good," he said aloud.

As he lumbered toward the door, Percy paused in front
of a mirror. He hardly recognized himself. His fur was stained
and matted, and his restless nap had left large, puffy bags
under both eyes. Out of habit, he looked around for his favorite
flannel pajamas.

"No," he muttered, shaking his head. "I don't need them."

The Arctic sun was as high and hot as it could be, so Percy stepped outside to warm himself. This time he moved slowly and carefully. "How does everybody manage?" he wondered. "This isn't very easy."

Percy soon realized that getting your feet stuck in the snow was very common. He also noticed several other bears with large dirty stains on their fur and big, puffy bags under their eyes.

"Everyone looks miserable," he thought. "Maybe all bears should wear pajamas." He quickly remembered, however, that his pajamas were only practically perfect. "I may be cold, dirty and tired," he said, "but at least now no one is laughing at me."

With renewed hope, Percy ran into a large crowd of bears roughhousing at the edge of the ice.

"Hey, Percy," one of the older bears shouted. "Where are your star-studded, flannel-footed peee-jays? Did ya lose 'em?"

"No!" said Percy. "I decided not to wear them today."

"My, oh my," mocked the oldest. "Percy's finally gonna act like a real bear."

"But I am...," Percy hesitated. "I *am* a real bear!"

"At least you're finally acting like one," said the others. "Come along and play with us today."

Percy smiled. "Perfect," he thought. "I'm part of the group." He bounced back and forth, grinning from ear to ear. "What are we playing?" he asked. "Freeze-tag? Leapfrog? Duck-duck-goose?"

The bears circled quietly, and Percy waited. Deep in the crowd, someone whispered softly, "1...2...3...Go!"

Suddenly Percy felt a powerful shove from behind and went tumbling toward the icy Arctic water. He barely had time to brace himself before the bitter cold seized him from nose to tail.

Stunned, Percy quickly gathered himself and swam to the surface. The other bears were laughing and pointing.

"Pretty fun game, eh, Percy?" said the biggest bear. "Where are your waterproof pj's when you really need them?"

Percy was crushed.

"I guess they just don't like me," he said, sinking into the slushy ice and dragging himself ashore. Never in his life had he been so cold and wet and lonely. All he could think about was the warmth and comfort of something friendly and familiar.

Looking up, Percy realized that he wasn't alone.

"Go on, fox, laugh away," he said. "I must be quite a funny sight."

But Aurora didn't laugh. "Hello, Percy," she said. "My name is Aurora. You don't know me, but I've been watching you for a long time. I miss seeing you in your splendid pajamas."

"You do?" Percy answered.

"Yes, of course," Aurora chimed. "The other bears are too dull. You always seem so happy in your pj's. I can't imagine why you'd go anywhere without them. They fit you perfectly!"

"Well, thank you," said Percy. "I thought the others might like me better if I didn't wear them."

"Oh, Percy," said Aurora kindly. "That's nonsense. They obviously don't know what they're missing. Follow me, I've got a great idea." The two of them headed toward Percy's den.

After discussing Aurora's plan on the walk home, Percy made an even bigger decision than the one that he'd made that morning.

They rushed inside and got right to work. Together, Percy and Aurora dug through mounds of flannel pajamas and sorted out the very best that Percy had to offer. Soon they had moved all of his pj's outside.

As they shook them out and folded them neatly on the snow, a small crowd gathered around.

"My goodness, stain resistant? These are very nice," said one bear.

"And these colors... Mmm, Mm. Very flattering," exclaimed a second.

"Someone has been living right!" whistled yet another bear. The sign that Percy and Aurora made said it all.

A day spent in THESE Perfect pj's is FAR better than a day spent without them. EVEN IF YOU DO LOOK A BIT SILLY SOMETIMES

Slowly but surely, the bears helped themselves. As Percy slipped once again into his own favorite pair, he knew Aurora was right.

Warm, happy, and wrapped in footed flannels, the two new friends looked proudly at the scene.

"So much for practically perfect," said Percy. "These pj's are positively perfect!"

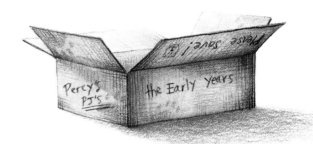